To Lily,
who takes me for a run every day.

VIKING
Published by Penguin Group
Penguin Young Readers Group, 345 Hudson Street, New York, New York 10014, U.S.A.
Penguin Group (Canada), 10 Alcorn Avenue, Toronto, Ontario, Canada M4V 3B2
(a division of Pearson Penguin Canada Inc.)
Penguin Books Ltd, 80 Strand, London WC2R 0RL, England
Penguin Ireland, 25 St Stephen's Green, Dublin 2, Ireland (a division of Penguin Books Ltd)
Penguin Group (Australia), 250 Camberwell Road, Camberwell,
Victoria 3124, Australia (a division of Pearson Australia Group Pty Ltd)
Penguin Books India Pvt Ltd, 11 Community Centre, Panchsheel Park, New Delhi – 110 017, India
Penguin Group (NZ), Cnr Airborne and Rosedale Roads, Albany, Auckland 1310, New Zealand
(a division of Pearson New Zealand Ltd)
Penguin Books (South Africa) (Pty) Ltd, 24 Sturdee Avenue, Rosebank, Johannesburg 2196, South Africa

Penguin Books Ltd, Registered Offices: 80 Strand, London WC2R 0RL, England.

First published in 2006 by Viking, a division of Penguin Young Readers Group

3 5 7 9 10 8 6 4

LIBRARY OF CONGRESS CATALOGING-IN-PUBLICATION DATA
Carlson, Nancy L.
Get up and go! / written and illustrated by Nancy Carlson.
p. cm.
Summary: Text and illustrations encourage readers, regardless of shape or size, to turn off the television
and play games, walk, dance, and engage in sports and other forms of exercise.
ISBN 0-670-05981-1 (hardcover)
[1. Exercise—Fiction. 2. Pigs—Fiction.] I. Title.
PZ7.C21665Ge 2006
[E]—dc22
2005003864

Manufactured in China
Set in Avenir
Book designed by Kelley McIntyre

You are special!

We all come in different shapes and sizes, and it doesn't

matter if you are tall, short, skinny, or round.

Your body is your own, and you need to take care of it!

So turn off the TV and get up and go exercise!

like your heart,

lungs
(keep them
smoke-free),

food you sometimes eat,

or a triple chocolate, caramel, marshmallow cream
sundae with extra whipped cream, and a cherry
on top.

when you hit a home run,

like a bag of chips

the stuff inside your body

bones,

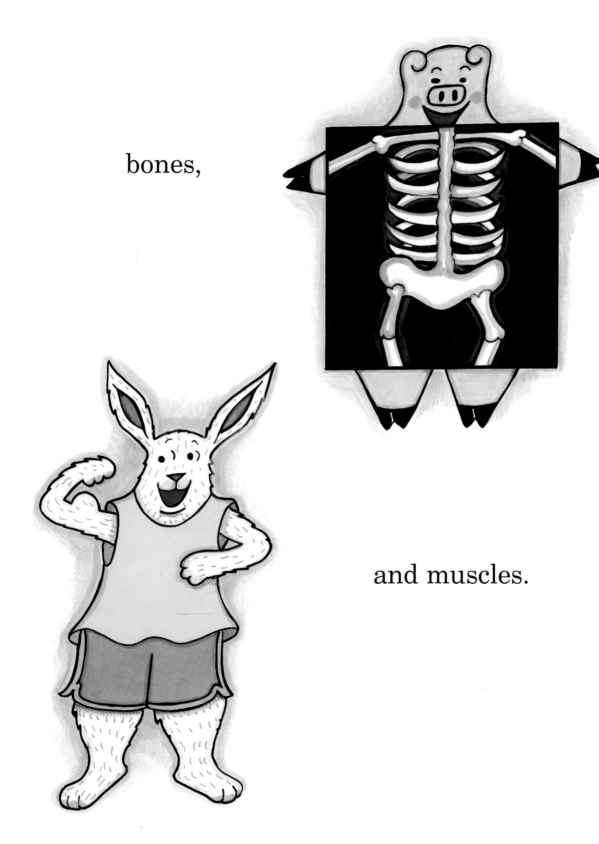

and muscles.

score a goal,

or can finally skate backward!

Exercise can help you become a better sport.

Because sometimes you might strike out,

lose the big game,

or—oops—fall down!

when you play tag at the park,

make new friends,

jump rope at school,

or just walk around the neighborhood!

when you go canoeing

or hiking in the woods,

or when you help your mom in the garden.

like to the top of a mountain,

to some amazing places

way down to the bottom of the sea,

or to the middle of nowhere!

When you're stuck babysitting your little brother . . .

turn up the music and get your heart pumping
by dancing. Today the living room . . .

someday Broadway!

So get to bed,

you pretty sleepy.

because who knows what will happen tomorrow . . .

when you get up and go exercise!